We're Going on a Ghost Hunt

by **Susan Pearson**   illustrated by **S. D. Schindler**

Amazon Children's Publishing

Text copyright © 2012 by Susan Pearson
Illustrations copyright © 2012 by S.D. Schindler

Amazon Publishing
Attn: Amazon Children's Books
P.O. Box 400818
Las Vegas, NV 89149
www.amazon.com/amazonchildrenspublishing

Library of Congress Cataloging-in-Publication Data

Pearson, Susan.
 We're going on a ghost hunt / by Susan Pearson ;
illustrated by S.D. Schindler. — 1st ed.
    p. cm.
 Summary: Children go out at night seeking a ghost,
through one scary place after another.
 ISBN 978-0-7614-6307-8 (hardcover) —
 ISBN 978-0-7614-6308-5 (ebook)
[1. Adventure and adventurers—Fiction. 2. Ghosts—
Fiction.] I. Schindler, S. D., ill. II. Title. III. Title: We
are going on a ghost hunt.
 PZ7.P323316Wf 2012   [E]—dc23   2011031815

The illustrations were rendered in watercolor,
gouache, and colored pencil.
Book design by Vera Soki
Editor: Margery Cuyler

Printed in China (w)
First edition
10 9 8 7 6 5 4 3 2 1

To Owen
—S.P.

To Eileen
—S.S.

We're going on a ghost hunt.
We're going to find a big one.
It's a starry night. The moon is bright.
We're not afraid.

Oh, no! What's this?
A muddy, murky swamp!
We can't go over it.
We can't go under it.
We'll have to go through it.

squish—
squash—
squoosh!

We're going on a ghost hunt.
We're going to find a big one.
It's a starry night. The moon is bright.
We're not afraid.

Oh, no! What's this?
A rustling, rattling cornfield.
We can't go over it.
We can't go under it.
We'll have to go through it.
Rustle-rustle-rat-a-tattle!

We're going on a ghost hunt.
We're going to find a big one.
It's a starry night. The moon is bright.
We're not afraid.

Oh, no! What's this?
A swishy, fishy river.
We can't go over it.
We can't go under it.
We'll have to go through it.
Do the dog paddle.
Do the back stroke.

SPLASH! SPLASH! SPLASH!

We're going on a ghost hunt.
We're going to find a big one.
It's a starry night. The moon is bright.
We're not afraid.

Oh, no! What's this?
The wild, windy woods.
We can't go over them.
We can't go under them.
We'll have to go through them.

TIPTOE . . . TIPTOE . . .

SHHHHH!

We're going on a ghost hunt.
We're going to find a big one.
It's a starry night. The moon is bright.
We're not afraid.

Oh, no! What's this?
A giant tree!
We can't go over it.
We can't go under it.
We'll have to climb up it.
What do you see?

We're going on a ghost hunt.
We're going to find a big one.
It's a starry night. The moon is bright.
We're not afraid.

Oh, no! What's this?
A graveyard!
We can't go over it.
We can't go under it.
We'll have to go through it.

IT'S A G-G-GHOST!
RUN! RUN! RUN!

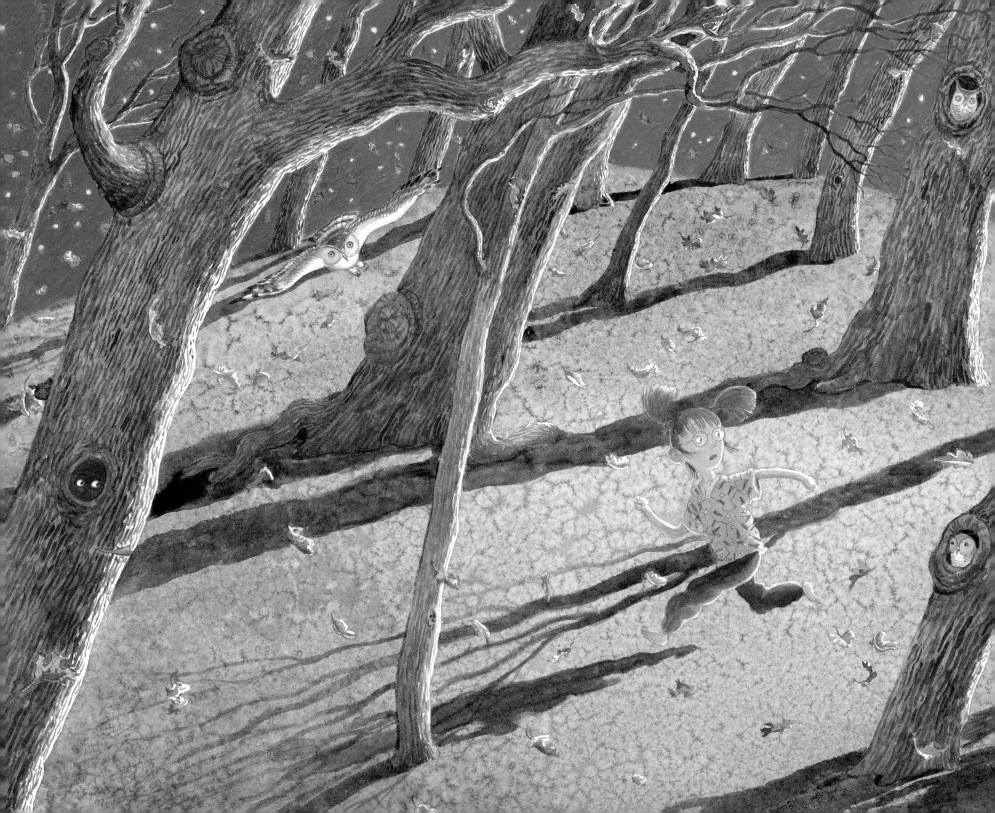

Forget the tree!
Back through the windy woods!
HOOO-HOOOOOO!
HOOOOOOOOO!

Back through the swishy, fishy river!
Stroke, stroke—fast, fast!
Paddle, paddle—faster, faster!

SPLASH! SPLASH! SPLASH!

Back through the rustling, rattling cornfield!

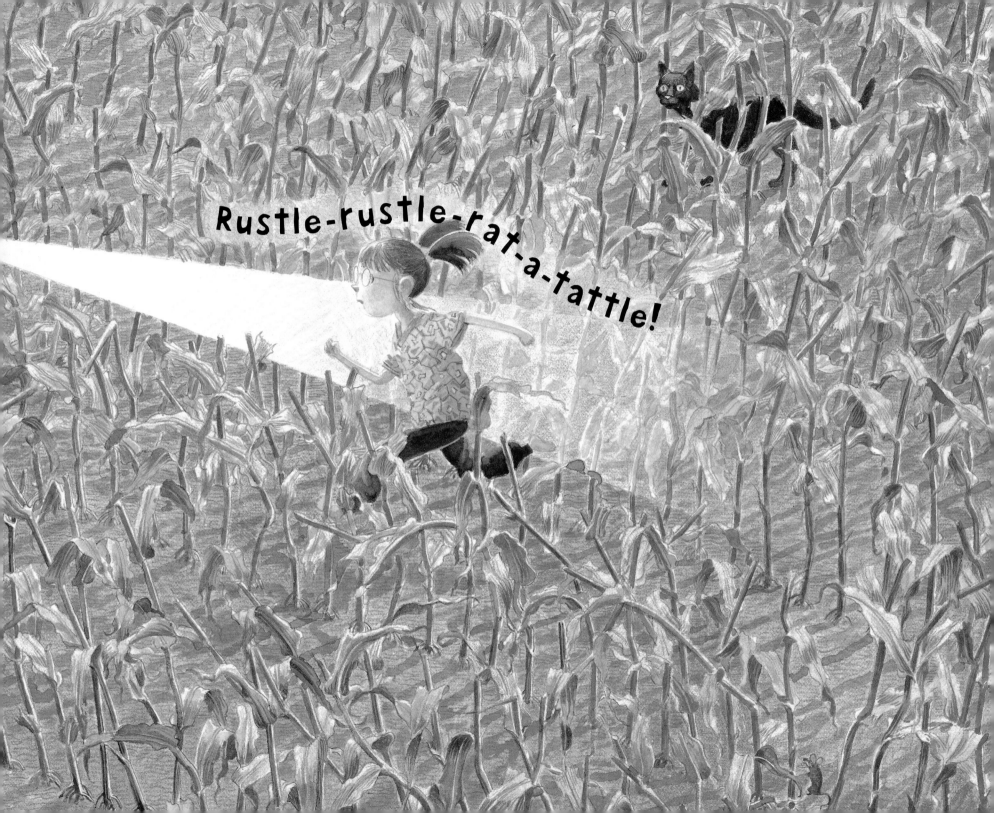

Back through the muddy, murky swamp.
squish—squash—squoosh!

Back into our house,

race up the stairs,

jump into bed,
get under the covers.
Where's my teddy bear? Grab him quick!
Cuddle up close,
safe from the ghost.

Ahhhhhhhhh!
We made it!

Let's go on a ghost hunt tomorrow!